STORYSACK

for Matthew and Freddie,
Ruby and Florence

Copyright © 2001 by Sandy Nightingale
Noddy character, car and image (page 9) © Enid Blyton Ltd., London.
May not be reproduced without permission.
The rights of Sandy Nightingale to be identified as the author and illustrator of this work
have been asserted by her in accordance with the Copyright, Designs and Patents Act, 1988.
First published in Great Britain in 2001 by Andersen Press Ltd., 20 Vauxhall Bridge Road, London SW1V 2SA.
Published in Australia by Random House Australia Pty., 20 Alfred Street, Milsons Point, Sydney, NSW 2061.
All rights reserved. Colour separated in Italy by Fotoriproduzione Beverari, Verona.
Printed and bound in Italy by Grafiche AZ, Verona.

10   9   8   7   6   5   4   3   2   1

British Library Cataloguing in Publication Data available.

ISBN 0 86264 899 8

This book has been printed on acid-free paper

THROWAWAY
BEAR

Sandy Nightingale

Ⓐ

Andersen Press
LONDON

It was spoilt Sophie's birthday and everyone gave her presents. Too many presents!

"Oh, not another teddy!" she complained, as she tore the wrapping paper from a beautiful, silky bear.

"Sophie, don't be so ungrateful," said her mother. "He's a lovely teddy. I'm sure he cost a lot of money."

"I don't care. I've got better teddies than him already," grumbled Sophie. "Next present!"

The poor teddy bear lay unwanted and ignored on the floor.

Nobody noticed when he was bundled up with all the wrapping paper and taken outside.

Nobody noticed when he was stuffed into the rubbish bin . . .

All night long he lay fretting, squashed amongst the wrapping paper in the dark, smelly bin.

Why had the little girl not liked him? Had they meant to throw him away? What would happen to him now?

There was nobody to talk to, nobody to ask, so he just wondered and waited, anxious and alone.

When morning came, it was with a crash and a clatter as the dustbin men arrived. The lid was lifted noisily from the bin.

"Hello, Mate," said the dustman in surprise. "You *are* a handsome bear. I reckon I've got just the place for you."

He tied Throwaway Bear to the front of his lorry amidst a jumble of other ornaments and toys.
There was hardly room for Bear.

The dustcart set off down the busy street. The engine rattled and roared as the lorry jerked along. And with every jerk, Throwaway Bear could feel the string around his middle getting looser.

Then everything happened at once. A dog ran out into the road, the lorry braked sharply and Throwaway Bear was flung high into the air. The dog snatched him up and bounded away through the gates of the park.

It didn't take long for the
dog to dig a deep hole.
He was just about to bury Bear,
like an old bone, when he heard
his master calling and he raced away.

But Throwaway Bear was not alone for long. A crowd of rabbits
had been watching from a safe distance. They sneaked up and
pounced on him, jostling and jeering, poking and prodding.
    "What's your name?"
    "Cat got your tongue?"
    "Let's tie him to a tree!"
    "He can be our prisoner!"
They were squabbling over who could tie the best knots when a
huge, black raven swooped down on them with a fearful screech.
            The startled rabbits scattered in all directions,
                    squealing at the tops of their voices.

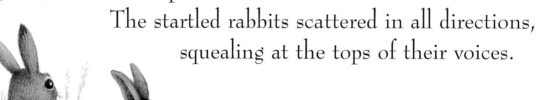

"Yeah, that's right! Hop it, you cowardly bullies!"
squawked the raven. He strutted over to Throwaway Bear.
"Well then, what have we got here? Something tasty, I hope."
And seizing Bear in his strong claws, he flew with him to the
top of a tree.

High in the swaying branches, the raven peered at his lunch.
He tried a couple of hopeful pecks.
"Kraa! Nothing but fluff and sawdust,"
he spat. Then he launched himself away
on angry black wings, sending poor
Bear sailing into the air.

Down he fell.

Down . . .

down . . .

down . . .

. . . until he plunged with a
loud SPLASH into the cold,
deep water of the lake.

Slowly he sank to the bottom and lay looking up through the
green water. He could see the weeds waving above his head and the
sunlight sparkling on the surface. Fish came to investigate, blowing
bubbles and mouthing silently at him. It was all very quiet and
dreamlike.

"This is where I'll stay forever," thought
Throwaway Bear sadly. "Nobody will ever
find me down here."

Then suddenly, through the sleepy silence,
he felt a sharp tug at the back of his neck.

There was a quick jerk, and he was being
pulled upwards through the water.

Bubbles rushed in his ears as he broke through
the surface, and he found himself whizzing
through the air again.

This time he landed on the grass,
in a dazed, muddy heap.

"Why, it's nothing but a scruffy old teddy bear!" exclaimed the fisherman, disappointed. "He'll be no use to anyone." And he packed up his fishing rods and went home in disgust.

Throwaway Bear lay sprawled on the bank, the fisherman's words ringing in his ears. It seemed a very long time ago that he had been a brand new birthday bear. And now it had come to this: "No use to anyone." It was unbearable.

But soon there was a new sound. It was a boy, laughing and chatting.

"It's a good thing Poppy's asleep," he was saying, "because she won't see me buy her birthday present."

"Yes," said his mum. "We should get a lovely present in the market. How about a hairslide or a bangle?"

There was no reply. The boy had spotted Throwaway Bear.

"Look, Mum!" he called. "Someone has lost their teddy."

"It doesn't look like a lost teddy to me," said his mum. "It looks like a dirty old thrown away teddy. Leave it alone, Paul."

"I want to take him home," said Paul, stubbornly. "Please, Mum. I've had such a brilliant idea."

So Bear was bundled into a plastic bag. He bumped along at Paul's side, wondering about the brilliant idea. What could it be?

When they reached the market, Paul made straight for the stall that sold ribbons and buttons and lace. "I need the longest piece of ribbon I can buy for fifty pence, please," he told the lady behind the counter.

"And what colour would you like?" asked the lady, kindly.

"Red," said Paul. "It's Poppy's favourite colour."

"What a good present," said Paul's mum. "Poppy will like that."

"There's going to be something else, as well . . ." said Paul, mysteriously.

"Mum, will you mend this teddy?"
Paul asked when they were home.
"He'd be a great bear if he were fixed."
Mum looked doubtfully at the
scruffy bear. "Hmm. I don't know,"
she said. "He really is in such a state."
"*Please*, Mum," begged Paul.
"*Please*, Mum," thought Bear, wishing hard.

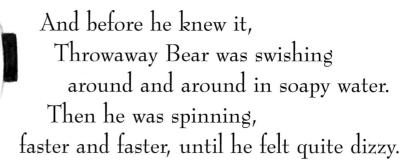

"Well, let's pop him into the washing
machine first," sighed Mum, giving in.

And before he knew it,
Throwaway Bear was swishing
around and around in soapy water.
Then he was spinning,
faster and faster, until he felt quite dizzy.

When the spinning stopped,
he was pegged to the washing line.
"He'll soon dry in this breeze,"
said Mum. "Then I'll have
another look at him."
"Hurry up and dry me, Breeze!"
thought Bear.

That evening, Mum got out her sewing basket.

"Now then, Ted, let's see what can be done with you," she said.

First, she sewed Bear's arm back on with strong, button thread. Next, she patched up all the rips and tears. She even pushed cotton wool into his foot where the stuffing had come out. Then she gave him a good brush until his coat shone.

"Now tie this ribbon around his neck," said Paul.

Mum smiled and tied a big bow. They both stared at Teddy.

"What a difference!" she said. "You were right, Paul. He's a beautiful teddy. You were clever to think of mending him."

"He's going to be Poppy's present," said Paul proudly. "Thanks for fixing him up, Mum."

So that was Paul's brilliant idea!

"But what if Poppy doesn't want me?" thought Throwaway Bear anxiously. "Will I be thrown away again?"

The next morning
was Poppy's birthday and
everyone gave her presents.

There was a tea set from
her mum and dad and a
picture book from her
grandma. She liked
everything.

Then Paul gave her
his present.

Poppy clapped her hands
with delight. "Bear!"
she cried, hugging him.
"Own Bear!"

Throwaway Bear could hardly
believe his fixed-up ears.

"Own Bear," he thought happily.
"Own Bear. Oh, I do like the sound
of that!"

And he was never, *ever,*
Throwaway Bear again.